Adrian at
LIBERTY

Adrian at

LIBERTY

MARIO HERBERT

ISBN 978-976-95594-5-5

Cover Art: The Search by Jeremy Marshall
Cover Design: Higher Definition Media

Redcore Publishing
Christ Church,
Barbados

CONTENTS

INTRODUCTION

This is the story of Adrian Manning, a sixteen-year-old boy whose secondary school life has been dotted with disaster. He has run afoul of his relentless, disciplinarian mother on many occasions. He has also run afoul of his 'follicly challenged' principal a fair share of times. Add to that list, jealous boyfriends, school bullies, street thugs and even his closest friends.

These disasters were chronicled in *Adrian at Large*, *Adrian at Last* and *Adrian at Loggerheads* but Adrian has matured—after coming to terms with his inner demons, Adrian is settled, focused and mostly at peace.

There are still some lingering demons to conquer, however, and just as gold must be refined in fire to achieve its true value, Adrian's road to true liberty will take him through fiery adversity.

What fiery trials await Adrian? What is the prize at the end of this fiery road of refinement?

Answers lie ahead, so turn the page and let the adventures begin!

ROLL BACK

Adrian sat on a worn bench next to a slightly leaning bus stop in the early morning breeze. As the wind rustled the tall grass on either side of the road, he checked his wristwatch restlessly, wondering how much longer his wait would be. With each passing vehicle, he was dichotomously eager for the wait to be over, and anxious about what would follow.

Suddenly, he heard the deep rumble of a diesel engine, and rose to his feet as a bus flew around the corner. As the bus approached the bus stop, adorned with airbrushed spoilers and blazing music, he was sure that his wait was over.

This thought was soon made fact as the bus reduced speed and a dark, slim but shapely girl jumped through the door in a white t-shirt and slim fitting blue jeans. She hit the sidewalk running, as the bus increased speed again and sped away without coming to a stop. The girl slowed herself to a halt by the time she reached Adrian, who stood watching her with his arms folded. Her neck was generously powdered, her lips were shining with lip gloss and her hair glistened in the sun, yielding its free will to a generous helping of hair gel.

"Sha'Tanya," said Adrian in a low voice, "why are you so late?"

"I was waiting on the bus," replied Sha'Tanya.

"Really now?" replied Adrian, with a quizzical but annoyed look. "Two buses came up from town since I was here."

"Error," said Sha'Tanya, rolling her eyes with attitude, "I only ride on buses with spoilers and music."

Adrian started to respond, then bit his lip as he turned away from Sha'Tanya and inhaled deeply.

"This way," he said, turning back towards Sha'Tanya with a fake smile as he gestured, "let's just get this over with."

"And here I thought you liked helping me, "replied Sha'Tanya, with attitude, as she started to follow in the direction Adrian had gestured.

"Look, I'm happy to let you use my computer," started Adrian, as he led Sha'Tanya away from the bus stop, "and I'm happy to assist you with your school assignments, but my mother is going to be home."

"Good stuff; I can finally get a proper introduction."

"There's nothing good about it!" cried Adrian, as he turned through a minor road and into a residential area. "She'll be peeping behind us."

"She can't be that bad," replied Sha'Tanya, rolling her eyes, "stop 'exabberating'."

"I am not exaggerating," said Adrian, intently, "she pops out from work to spy on me in town after school and she calls my teachers and the neighbours to keep tabs on me."

Adrian gestured to the nicely painted wooden houses on either side of the old, but well-kept road.

"Her agents are probably peeping through curtains as we speak," he said, "it's like she's always convinced I'm up to something."

"Hmm," started Sha'Tanya, "I wonder why she would think that."

"Stop being sarcastic," said Adrian, staring intently at Sha'Tanya.

"Just saying," started Sha'Tanya, throwing up her hands in a defensive stance, "I was there a time she chased you …"

"Then you know she stops at nothing short of the law," interrupted Adrian, "nothing and no one stops her …"

"As I was saying," cried Sha'Tanya, forcefully, "I was there a time she chased you, and the word in the school was that you deserved it."

"I haven't been in trouble in three terms. I'm a fifth-former now, settled, and at the top of my class; I'm a very different person but she can't see it."

A couple minutes later, they arrived at Adrian's home. It was a little wood and brick structure, painted white, with purple trimmings and a porch to the front. Adrian and his guest climbed the steps into the porch to find a note attached to the front door. Adrian snatched the note off the door and started to read it intently.

"Well…" said Sha'Tanya, impatiently.

"My mother's left home," said Adrian, with a puzzled look on his face, "said a neighbour gave her a lift to town to do some shopping."

"So, let me get this straight," said Sha'Tanya, smiling as she put her arm around Adrian's neck, "your mother's suspicious of you, but she's cool 'bout you being home alone with a girl she ain't even meet yet?"

"It's a trick," said Adrian, as he retrieved a key from under the outdoor welcome mat.

"Really now?" asked Sha'Tanya, laughing.

"I'm telling you, it's a trick," replied Adrian, as he unlocked the door, "she's like a spy satellite; you don't see her, but she has eyes on your every movement."

The teenagers entered the living room, which was a flushed, shared space with the dining room and the kitchen, with imaginary divisions. There was a partition to the left, separating two bedrooms and a bathroom from the shared space. Adrian started searching the living room, pulling the cushions out of the burgundy upholstered suite, and checking underneath the chairs and centre table.

"What exactly you expecting to find?" asked Sha'Tanya, with her hands on her hips.

"I don't know yet," cried Adrian, "some kind of listening device, maybe; there's got to be a trap here somewhere."

When Adrian returned the cushions to the chair, Sha'Tanya sat in the single-seater and began to examine her nails as Adrian moved into the dining room.

"Aren't you going to help me?" asked Adrian, as he

looked under the dining table and chairs.

"Error," Sha'Tanya replied, calmly, as she retrieved a retractable file from her pocket and proceeded to file her nails.

Adrian concluded his survey of the dining set and moved to the bookshelf against the right wall of the dining room. After checking behind numerous books to no avail, his eyes fell on a big book—the biggest book on the bookshelf. Adrian pulled the book, titled *101 Health Conditions*, off the shelf, sure that he would find something behind it, but there was nothing but an old letter.

Disappointed and confused, he then turned his attention to his bedroom on the left. Adrian had a small bedroom, but it felt spacious by virtue of a single, twin-sized bed, and the placement of the items in the room—a small computer workstation and a chest of drawers.

Adrian rushed into the room, examined the computer workstation and then turned his attention to the chest of drawers, which featured a small assortment of cosmetics and a piggybank in the shape of a shark. With nothing suspicious found thus far, Adrian was about to go through the drawers of the chest, when he glanced around to his bed and stood frozen at the sight before him—a pair of rollerblades.

In that moment, the room faded away, as well as the house and his guest. As his current reality melted away, it was replaced by a vivid memory of the events surrounding the last time he had seen those rollerblades— just over four years ago.

At that time, Adrian had just entered secondary school and had just made a new friend—a clear, slim boy, of average height with a speed hump in the bridge of his nose—named Jay. It was the first Wednesday of his first term in first form, and he was sitting on a bench with Jay, eating his lunch as a dark girl passed by and shook his world. She was slim, but shapely, and that shape was accentuated by a uniform which was tighter than the cork of a wine bottle. It would be two years before he would find out her name—Sha'Tanya. It would also be two years before his crush on her would be shattered, but at that moment, on that bench, she was the most stunning person in his world.

"Stop drooling," said Jay, to a mesmerised Adrian, "she's not even that pretty."

"I'm not drooling," cried Adrian, defensively, "and it doesn't matter how pretty you think she is, she's just so ..."

"Breath-taking?"

"Striking," said Adrian, emphatically, "look how shiny her hair is."

"Don't be fooled," said Jay, with a laugh, "that's hair gel, and the amount she's using, her hair is pretty but stiff as raw spaghetti."

"Bite your tongue," cried Adrian, staring at Jay intently, "I won't have you speaking negatively about this African goddess."

"That 'African goddess' walked past you like you didn't exist," cried Jay, falling off the bench with laughter, "she's clearly a popular girl and you're a member of the chess club; girls like her don't notice boys like you, so you might as well get used to it."

In that moment, as Jay laughed, Adrian was inundated with a flood of emotions—shame, sadness and anger all rolled into one. He was resolute that he would never get used to being unnoticed, and without saying a word to his still laughing friend, his brain started churning to hatch a plan to rectify his situation.

He needed something to set him apart from other students. As a gift for passing his secondary school entrance examination, his mother had promised to get him a Gladiator 64 portable gaming console at launch; that would surely do the trick, but it wasn't going to launch till the following year. He needed something right at that moment, to cement his noticeability early in his school life.

Suddenly, an idea hit him like a cold hand. It was a crazy idea, but it was the only idea he had—he was going to rollerblade to school.

The next morning, Adrian's mother had a doctor's appointment, and left home earlier than usual. Adrian packed his rollerblades and his helmet in his school backpack, opting to leave some of his school books at home. He left home a little earlier than usual to go into town. Once there, he didn't take his regular bus to school; he caught one that put him close enough to skate the rest of the way.

Adrian watched the bus drive away after disembarking, and then sat on a bench at the bus stop on the side of a busy road, with an industrial complex behind him, and a residential area on the other side. He took his skates and helmet out of his backpack, removed his shoes and started to prep himself for the skate to school. In short order, he had secured his school shoes in his backpack, fastened his skates and helmet and stood at a zebra crossing, near the bus stop.

A bus which was headed for the city, stopped at the crossing, allowing him to cross to the residential area on the other side of the road. As Adrian skated across the road, he caught a glimpse of a familiar face in the bus—his mother. It was as if Adrian died for a couple of seconds; that glimpse of his mother's face halted his natural bodily functions. His bodily functions soon returned but there was a persistent burning in his gut as he completed his crossing and dashed through the residential area.

"Did she see me?" he pondered. "If she did, she'll destroy me when I get back home—but she can't take away the status I'm about to gain at school."

Adrian resolved to focus on the execution of the mission at hand, and worry about possible consequences later. The road was recently paved and there was no traffic in the residential area, so he was able to zip through it safely and relatively quickly.

"Thank God for that cross-country run we did yesterday for physical education," he thought to himself as he skated along, "it taught me all of these roads."

Fifteen minutes later, Adrian was rolling through the school gate with pride and purpose. As he came up the worn driveway into the school, he could see many children congregated on and around benches at the front of the school, near the office block. They were already starting to notice him, and he could see many of them pointing in his direction as he approached.

"So, Jay thinks I'm destined to be unnoticed, does he?" he said to himself as he approached the children.

As Adrian reached the area where the children were gathered, he did a twirl on the skates and brought himself to a halt. There was a lot of commotion as he unfastened his helmet.

"What the bird," cried one boy, "I've never seen anyone rollerblade to school."

"You' so lucky," cried a girl in the crowd, "my mother would never let me do that."

Adrian scanned the crowd, hoping to see his African goddess, but she wasn't there. He was still basking in all the attention he was receiving but his mind wasn't focusing on any of the individual comments; they all congealed into ambient chatter. His mind was focused on the African goddess and he was preparing to roll deeper into the school in hopes that she would see him—until a deep voice shattered both the chatter and his thoughts.

"That is far enough!" boomed the voice.

Adrian spun around to investigate the source of the voice, to see a tall, slender, clear skinned man, with an Adam's apple the size of a small goitre, and a hairline receding towards extinction; it was the principal, Wilberforce Harding.

"I can't stop you from skating to school," he continued, "but there will be no skating into the compound beyond this point; remove the skates—or they will be removed."

Adrian promptly did as the principal ordered; he

didn't want to get into trouble in his first week, and he definitely didn't want the skates to be confiscated. By the time he had packed away the skates, the bell had rung for morning assembly, and he made his way to the assembly hall with the other children.

"I still got great mileage out of my stunt," he thought, as he passed under a long trellis and mounted the steps leading to the hall entrance, "word will spread about my entrance this morning and this will all be worth it—even if my mother destroys me this evening."

By the time assembly ended, Adrian was still upbeat. As he exited the hall, he was excited for the day ahead of him, anxious to see how quickly word would spread—until he saw a truly horrifying sight. There was a big, brown, cruel-looking woman in a white pantsuit, under the trellis, marching up the walkway to the hall; it was his mother, and she was holding a large belt. Evidently, her doctor's appointment was on the route of the bus Adrian had taken, and on her way back to town, she did indeed see him cross the road.

It was as if Adrian died again, this time for a couple more seconds. His body seemed to shut down; everything except his wide eyes, pounding heart, and his stomach, which lit up like a cane fire. He could see his mother approaching but he was frozen in position; his feet didn't work. Then he heard the voice of a male student behind him.

"Hold up, men, this looks like action."

This was the jolt of electricity needed to resuscitate his bodily functions.

"She must have disembarked at the next bus stop and found her way here," Adrian thought, as his mother's hulking form approached him, "I don't know where she got that belt from but I know there's no way I'm going to be flogged by my mother at school."

Adrian turned and took flight westward, past the staff room and towards the hardcourt in the middle of the school, with his mother promptly engaging in hot pursuit and an eruption of gasps and chuckles from the student body.

"How'd this parent get in the school?" came the cry of a teacher as Adrian dashed past the staff room. "Somebody, call the guard!"

Adrian figured the guard might be able to stop his mother, but not before he endured considerable humiliation.

"This is not the way I wanted to be noticed," he thought, overtaken with shame and feeling the weight of his backpack. His mother's size should have put him at an advantage but his backpack felt like a small human clinging to his back, preventing him from reaching his true speed.

By the time he reached the hardcourt, she had actually gained on him, and Adrian knew he had to lose the backpack to have any chance of survival. However, he wasn't about to leave his bag unattended with his rollerblades inside, and he didn't have time to affix his padlock.

Adrian darted across the hardcourt, which was surrounded by four, two-story classroom blocks, and headed for a staircase to the left of the block directly facing him. As he moved across the court with his human-weighted backpack and his huge mother in hot pursuit, Adrian felt like a Jet Ski lugging a water skier at close range, pursued by a tugboat, which was somehow keeping up. As he zeroed in on the staircase, children parted like ocean waves at the behest of the Jet Ski and the tugboat. Adrian dashed up the staircase, feeling the weight of the skier attached to his back even more than before. As he entered the one-hundred-and-eighty-degree angle in the middle of the staircase, he glanced backwards to see the tugboat maintaining pace in the wake of the parted waves.

"I can't be caught, I can't be caught," he thought, as he approached the top of the stairwell, with his heart pounding like a two-hundred-horsepower engine.

The bell rang, signalling the first period, just as he reached the top of the stairs. He darted to the right, along a narrow corridor which adjoined that block to the southern block. As he turned the right-angle onto the southern block, he saw his friend, Jay, mounting the top step at the far end of the corridor.

"Finally!" he thought to himself, as he fixed his eyes on Jay with tunnel vision.

The Jet Ski sped down the narrow canal, splashing waves of students against the railing on the left and the classroom walls on the right. The tugboat was not far behind and by this time, teachers were downstairs on the hardcourt, with a dark, overweight guard, looking up with curiosity and questioning bystanders. Adrian noticed the teachers and the guard, and he could hear his mother not too far behind him, but he reaffixed his vision on Jay. His mother was more determined than he had ever seen her and he couldn't rely on the staff to stop her. He removed his backpack as he approached Jay and mustered all his strength to throw it at Jay.

"Hold this for me!" he shouted, ignoring the shock and puzzlement etched upon Jay's face as he struggled to manage the weight of his catch.

Finally, the weight was lifted; the skier fell off and the Jet Ski was free to push every bit of horsepower to the task of escaping the tugboat. Adrian dashed down the stairs, leading back to the eastern end of the hard-court, feeling lighter than ever and jumping three steps at a time. As his foot was about to hit the step, he saw the guard, flanked by a group of teachers at the end of the staircase, bidding him to stop. They were like the coast guard but Adrian wasn't about to be stopped—not after finally getting rid of the backpack. The engine in his chest went into overdrive and the Jet Ski jumped through the air, over the right-side railing of the stair-case and landed on the edge of the hard court.

As Adrian recovered from his landing, the coast guard was scattering as the tugboat pushed through at full steam.

"They don't pay me enough for this," he heard a teacher cry, as he steadied himself to resume his run.

The chase continued in short order as the liberated Jet Ski sped back towards the hall, followed by the tug-boat and the overweight coast guard patrol vessel. The chase had gone full circle—from the hall and back—and Adrian was pondering where it could realistically go from there. As he sped past the hall, with freedom from the backpack, he started to distance himself from his pursuers. He was feeling winded but upbeat, when suddenly he saw a sight that shook him to his core; coming up the pathway under the trellis was his African goddess, now getting to school.

"This isn't how I wanted her to see me," Adrian thought, as he turned to run down the same pathway, under the trellis.

"Excuse me," said Adrian, as he flew past her, trying to hold his head down.

He could hear his mother's voice behind him in the distance, "Get out of the way, little girl."

As he continued to fly down the pathway, towards the office block, he heard the voice of his African goddess for the first time, in the distance.

"Who you calling 'little girl'?" she shouted. "Error!"

As Adrian approached the office block, he could see some workmen servicing the air conditioning system. The windows to the principal's office were open and knowing that the chase couldn't go on indefinitely, he made a shocking decision; he ran straight towards the principal's office and dove through the bottom of one of the open sash windows.

Once in the principal's office, Adrian quickly picked himself up off the floor and stood before the principal himself, who was sitting behind a big desk, staring at him intently with his arms folded.

"Sorry for the intrusion, Principal Harding," he said quickly, before the principal could speak, "my name is Adrian Manning and I really need you to flog me—right now."

"What?" cried the principal, with consternation etched upon his face. "Why should I flog you?"

"Because it's better than the alternative …"

At that moment, Adrian's mother came hurtling through the window, belt in hand, but her midsection failed to clear the window frame—she was stuck.

Mr. Harding jumped up from his chair.

"What is this madness?" he cried.

"You don't have to flog me, Mum," said Adrian, outstretching his hands towards his mother in a halting gesture, and ignoring the principal's question as his mother fought to free herself from the window frame, "Mr. Harding was just about to do the honours."

"Cease and settle!" cried the principal, as Adrian's mother popped free and landed on the floor with a thud.

As his mother picked herself up off the floor, Adrian saw the fire in her eyes, and with a racing heart, he instinctively started to run towards the door, still looking back at his pursuer.

"Stop!" cried both adults, simultaneously, as Adrian turned his head away from them to see that he was running straight into a closed door. There was no time to react; Adrian slammed into the door, headfirst, and instantly blacked out.

The next thing Adrian remembered was waking up in a twin-sized bed, in a small room he presumed to be the school sickbay. The principal was standing at his bedside, along with his mother, the overweight guard and a dark lady in white, whom he presumed to be a nurse—but was actually the guidance counsellor.

"What happened?" asked Adrian, groggily.

"You hit your head," said Mr. Harding.

"I did?" asked Adrian, with a perplexed look. "That would explain why my head is pounding and the room is spinning."

"You really don't remember hitting your head?" asked the counsellor.

"The last thing I remember is skating to school," said Adrian.

"Sounds like you have a concussion."

"You can drop the act now," cried his mother, gripping the belt at both ends with either hand, "or I will bring your memory back with a lash."

The counsellor gasped as the principal extended his hand, gripping the middle of the belt firmly, with a stern look on his face.

"You should be ashamed of yourself, woman," cried the counsellor, folding her arms.

"Now I see why he preferred me to flog him," said the principal, "this is no way to treat a child."

"I know you're probably frustrated by his behaviour," continued the counsellor, "but you have to realise that behaviour is often not the problem, but a symptom of the real, internal problem; your energy might be better spent trying to figure out what's happening emotionally and psychologically inside this boy!"

Adrian's mother stared at him with fire in her eyes.

"I know you're faking this," she said, looking at Adrian, sternly, "but you win this one."

ROLL BACK

At that moment there was a loud banging sound which jolted Adrian clear out of his memory-driven daze. He was back to his present-day reality—standing in his room, looking at the rollerblades on his bed as his houseguest, Sha'Tanya, banged on his bedroom door.

"Earth to Adrian," said Sha'Tanya, staring intently at him, "you supposed to be helping me do my project on the computer and you in here staring at skates."

"Four years ago, I took these rollerblades to school," said Adrian, as he took the skates up off the bed, "and my mother confiscated them as punishment."

"So, what, you happy to get them back?" asked Sha'Tanya, with a puzzled look on her face. "You can't get your feet in those skates now!"

"You don't understand," cried Adrian, emotionally, "it's not the skates I'm getting back."

Sha'Tanya just gave him a blank stare.

"When my mother took these skates four years ago," said Adrian, trying to fight the water that was settling in his eyes, "she said that I would get them back when she trusted me again."

"Wow, that's so beautiful!" cried, Sha'Tanya, putting her arm around Adrian's shoulder as he dried his eyes, "she ain't trying to trap you; she left you home alone because she trusts you again."

Adrian turned his head and locked eyes with Sha'Tanya for a couple of seconds.

"What?" she asked.

"Having established that my mother finally trusts me again," he said, softly, "do you really think this is an appropriate time and place to put the moves on me?"

Sha'Tanya removed her arm and stepped back, giving Adrian a cold stare.

"You thought I was putting the moves on you?" she said, placing her hands on her hips. "Rewind and come again because that is an error!"

PASS MARK

Adrian walked on a worn, cracked road, through a sea of government-run attached apartment blocks in the late morning sun, in a blue t-shirt and khaki short pants, with his backpack behind him. He was on his way to his friend, Sha'Tanya's house, to tutor her in preparation for a physics test. As he followed the directions to his friend's house, he passed through a sea of late morning activity—from men playing dominoes to children riding bicycles. His nostrils were attacked by different scents, both pleasant and unpleasant—from marijuana smoke to pots of stew. These scents and activities mirrored the dichotomy of active emotions he felt within him. On the one hand, he was excited, as it was the first time Sha'Tanya had ever consented to him seeing her house, and meeting members of her family. On the other hand, he had assisted Sha'Tanya with her school work before, and while it was somewhat rewarding, it wasn't easy. On this particular day, he wasn't looking forward to a repeat.

Nevertheless, he had resolved to do the best he could, undergirded by the knowledge that she really needed the help. As he approached what he presumed to be Sha'Tanya's apartment, he could hear their physics teacher's deep voice echoing in his head.

"Jerome Atkins … zero. Akanni Johnson … five out of fifty. Sha'Tanya Carter … nine out of fifty."

These were the first three results disclosed after their last test, and Adrian felt sorry for Sha'Tanya. As he walked up to the door of the narrow, two-story unit, he took a long, deep breath and tried to prepare himself mentally for the task ahead.

Adrian mounted the steps and knocked at the door three times; there was no answer.

"Good morning!" he called out, aloud, before repeating his knock.

This time, a dark, old woman with grey cornrowed hair appeared at the window.

"Good morning, I'm here to see …" started Adrian, stopping short at the sight of a chamber pot rising.

Before Adrian knew what was happening, a flood of urine came raining down out of the chamber pot, and onto him.

As he tried to process what had just happened to him, the door flew open and a dark girl stood in the doorway looking at him with her mouth open. She was slim but quite shapely, wearing a white t-shirt and very short, damaged jeans. Her hair was stuck to her head with what seemed like half a bottle of gel—it was Sha'Tanya.

"What the bird," she cried, "Adrian, I' so sorry!"

"Sorry?" cried Adrian, coming to terms with what had just soaked him. "That doesn't begin to fix this!"

"Come in the house, quick," Sha'Tanya replied, "give me a chance to fix this."

Adrian promptly stepped through the door to find himself in a cosy living room. There was a staircase behind the living room, followed by a small dining room, which Adrian could only see a glimpse of, behind the staircase. There was a slim, fragile-looking old lady seated in the sofa of a mahogany suite, examining him intently with her gaze.

"Who is this?" cried the old lady, "I thought that was the door-to-door salesman that keep asking me for money."

"Error!" cried Sha'Tanya. "This is my friend, Adrian, and the salesman keeps asking you for money because you owe him money!"

"I don't remember that."

"You don't remember a lot of things. I told you my friend, Adrian, was coming here to help me study for my test," cried Sha'Tanya, gesturing angrily, "and we told you a thousand times to stop throwing pee on people!"

As this was happening, Adrian was evaluating the damage; the front of his t-shirt and short pants were wet with urine, as were the straps of his backpack. His attention was suddenly drawn away from his clothes, however, as a female voice came booming from upstairs.

"Granny throwing pee on people again?"

"Yes," shouted Sha'Tanya to the unseen voice upstairs, "on my friend, Adrian!"

"That's the same pee she had storing up from last weekend?" returned the voice.

"Yes," shouted the old woman, "now I gotta start from scratch!"

"Hold up, wait a minute," cried Adrian, wanting to rip his clothes—and his skin—from his body, "did she say 'last weekend'?"

"Be cool," replied Sha'Tanya, quickly, "follow me; let me get you cleaned up."

Sha'Tanya led Adrian past the staircase and into a room which doubled as a dining room and kitchen. There was a small, four burner stove, a small fridge and a single L-shaped counter with a toaster oven and a sink, set over cupboards. With the kitchen counter and appliances, there was just enough space left in the room to hold a wrought iron, six-seater dining set. She led him around the table to a door on the right of the room, which she opened to reveal a bathroom.

"Take off that shirt and pants," she said, "I' coming back with a fresh towel; you can shower while I wash the clothes for you."

Adrian entered the small, cramped bathroom and was instantly presented with a sight which made him quite uneasy; there were lady's undergarments hung over the top of the shower curtain, around the shower head and shower faucet.

"What have I gotten myself into?" Adrian pondered.

He wanted to abort the mission, but he couldn't ride the bus in his current state, so he went along with the plan. Dropping his backpack on the floor, he removed his shirt and pants and surrendered them to Sha'Tanya through the partially closed door, receiving in like manner, a towel, alternative clothing and a strong deodorant spray for the straps of his backpack. He didn't examine his new threads; he took to the shower immediately, anxious to sanitise his epidermis. With the intimate garments hung all around him, however, he didn't wish to be in there a minute longer than he needed to, so he finished his shower in five minutes. He then promptly exited the shower and headed for his replacement garments, feeling relieved that the unpleasant ordeal was coming to an end—until he saw the clothes Sha'Tanya had brought for him.

"You've got to be kidding me," he said, under his breath, as he stared in disbelief at the garments he was expected to wear; they were almost identical to what Sha'Tanya was wearing.

With no other options available, Adrian put on the short t-shirt, leaving his navel exposed, and then squeezed into the jeans with great effort. He then opened the bathroom door to see Sha'Tanya sitting at the dining table with her books. He made his way to the table with his backpack in hand, taking very small steps so as not to rip the tiny pants, which was covering less than a third of his legs.

"I will find a way to make this up to you," said Sha'Tanya, softly, with a guilty look on her face, as Adrian took a seat next to her.

"The best way you can make it up to me is to pass this test," said Adrian, trying to overlook the embarrassment he felt, "what do you know about Newton's first law of motion?"

"An object in motion …"

"Yes …"

"Will continue to be in the same state unless acted upon by an external force."

"Wow!" cried Adrian. "That's absolutely correct."

"I ain't know what a word of that means though, I just have a good memory," said Sha'Tanya, in a low defeated tone. "I remember Mr. Garnett saying that a lot in class."

"Okay," said Adrian, holding his head, "it's talking about inertia."

"Inner-what?"

"Not inner-anything—inertia," said Adrian, "the resistance of a body to changes in momentum."

"Sorry, Adrian," cried Sha'Tanya, jumping up from the table, "this is a big jumbled mess in my head."

"Wait," cried Adrian, jumping up and holding her by the arms, "don't give up on yourself; you can understand this."

"This is the only subject I failed last year, and everybody in my 'fambily' failed physics," she said in an exasperated tone, "maybe we just ain't cut out for physics."

"I don't know 'bout your family, but you are," cried Adrian, triumphantly, "you use it every day."

Adrian looked at Sha'Tanya with a wide smile, as his brain churned.

"You jump out of buses a lot," he said, "I've seen you do it."

"Yeah …" she replied, in a sceptical manner, "only sissies wait for the bus to stop—no offense to you."

"I'll ignore that last comment," said Adrian, sternly, before continuing. "What do you do after jumping out of the bus?"

"Hit the ground running …"

"Why?"

"Because if I don't, I' gonna fall and burst my face."

"That's inertia!" said Adrian, excitedly.

"Explain," Sha'Tanya replied, with a look of intrigue.

"The bus is moving, so it has momentum, and you are in it, so you have momentum as well," started Adrian, with a gleam in his eyes, "when you jump out of the bus, you still carry that momentum; your body doesn't change state."

"The resistance of a body to changes in momentum …" said Sha'Tanya, as her face started to light up.

"Exactly! The ground is not moving, it has no momentum, but you do," Adrian continued, "so if you just jump from the bus and try to stick a landing …"

"My body would resist the change and I would fall forward!" cried Sha'Tanya, excitedly.

"And that's why you hit the ground running—to maintain the momentum your body expects."

Sha'Tanya threw both arms around Adrian's neck and hugged him tightly.

"Thanks for believing in me," she said, giving Adrian a kiss on the cheek, "nobody ever believed that I can excel at this kind of thing."

As the tutoring session continued, Adrian was up-beat, and hopeful that the hardships and embarrass-ment of that morning would all be worth it—but the test would be the ultimate gauge.

Several days later, the moment of truth came. Adri-an and Sha'Tanya sat side by side in the back row of their classroom, awaiting the results of their latest test. At the top of the class, a young, lanky man of medium complexion sat on the edge of a big teacher's desk, fac-ing the class with a stack of papers in his hand; this was Mr. Garnett, the hip, new physics teacher.

"As usual, we're gonna start from the bottom and come up," said Mr. Garnett.

Anxiety erupted in Adrian's stomach, not for him-self, as he was sure of his performance in the test, but for Sha'Tanya. He still had nightmares about that chamber pot, and for Sha'Tanya to fail again, his entire ordeal would have been for naught.

"The marks, out of fifty, are as follows," started the teacher, "Jerome Atkins ... zero!"

The class collectively burst into laughter, as a pale, white boy, with a thin frame reminiscent of a stick in-sect, walked up to the teacher to collect his paper. This was the way every physics test-results session started, but the predictability of it never seemed to lessen the hilarity for Adrian and his classmates.

"Akanni Johnson," continued the teacher, "twelve!"

A dark, thick-lipped Rastafarian of average height and build, rose to his feet, taking a bow before ap-proaching the teacher. The class erupted in a chorus of cheers and laughter.

As the teacher prepared to call the next name, Adrian and Sha'Tanya made eye contact. He could only imagine the anxiety she must have been feeling, several magnitudes higher than his own.

"Richelle Clarke," continued the teacher, "twenty-five out of fifty!"

"You passed," whispered Adrian to Sha'Tanya, with wide eyes as he tried to subdue his excitement.

Several names later, the teacher revealed the information he so anxiously awaited.

"Sha'Tanya Carter," said the teacher, as a hush engulfed the room, "forty!"

The class erupted in applause as Sha'Tanya rose to her feet with a beaming face. As she made her way to the teacher, her classmates all rose to their feet as they continued to clap. As Sha'Tanya took the paper from Mr. Garnett, her beaming smile gave way to tears, which was highly unusual for her.

"Listen up, everybody," she said, turning to face the class, "I really want to big-up Adrian for helping me understand this stuff; I never thought I could get a score like this."

In that moment, as Adrian saw how much the score meant to Sha'Tanya, everything he had gone through to tutor her was well worth it.

The teacher praised Adrian for assisting his fellow classmate, before going on to reveal that he had scored fifty out of fifty on the test.

The rest of the period was used to go through corrections for the test. At the end of the period, as Mr.

Garnett exited the class, he had a message for Adrian.

"One more thing," he said, as he was about to go through the door, "maybe Adrian can consider helping Jerome and Akanni as well."

"That ain't a bad idea," said Sha'Tanya to Adrian.

"Let me put this in terms you will understand," he replied, giving her a cold stare. "Error!"

"Oh, come on, Adrian, I know you and Akanni ain't friends but at least think 'bout helping Jerome; that poor boy's stuck at zero."

"He's hardly stuck; he made it to fifth form," started Adrian, in an agitated tone, "his family is loaded."

"Their money could get him promoted, but your tutoring skills could get him some self-respect."

"Tutoring is not easy," started Adrian, in a low but still agitated tone, "I didn't help you because I like tutoring; I helped you because I like you."

"You don't have to like me to help me," interrupted a voice, "you just have to like money."

Adrian and Sha'Tanya looked around to see Jerome, standing and staring at Adrian with shiny blue eyes.

"Help me do half-decent on next week's test," said Jerome, with a gleam in his eyes, "and there's a hundred dollars with your name on it."

Adrian looked at Jerome with a gleam in his eyes. He had seen Jerome chauffeured to school in a Mercedes Benz on multiple occasions, and he'd always known him to blame his maid for failing to pack the correct books for school; Adrian was sure he could and would pay his debt as promised.

"You've got a deal," said Adrian, extending his hand

towards Jerome, "just tell me when and where."

"This weekend," replied Jerome, accepting the handshake, "at my house; I need my parents to believe … I mean, to see that I'm making an effort."

At that moment, the teacher for their next class entered the room and Jerome released Adrian's hand and turned to return to his seat.

"Oh, one more thing," he said, quickly turning his head back to Adrian, "my chauffeur won't be available so you'll have to make your way there."

By the end of that school day, Adrian had recorded Jerome's address, and made plans for the money.

The weekend came and Adrian was up early and on his way to Jerome's house with his backpack, in long, blue jeans and an orange t-shirt. His mother had advised him on the appropriate bus to take and he had asked the conductor to put him off at the appropriate point; that point came about forty-five minutes into his journey.

"You sure this is the right place?" he asked the conductor as he disembarked the bus, "all I can see is bush."

The dark, thin conductor pointed indifferently to a winding hill, about a kilometre long, leading to a bevy of massive houses in the distance.

"Of course," he thought to himself, as the bus drove off, "there's no need for buses in an area as affluent as that; these people have chauffeurs."

Adrian's heart sank as he began his kilometre-long journey up the hill. Fortunately, his backpack was light and the majority of the hill was a mild slope, only becoming steep for the last twenty-five metres. Unfortunately, the monotony of the terrain threatened to send him into a comma early on. The only thing he could do to preserve his sanity was to let his mind wander— away from the monotonous journey and to the events which led him to it. He remembered vividly, the ordeal he had experienced at Sha'Tanya's house. However, as traumatic as it was, the moment that kept echoing in his mind was something he had said to Sha'Tanya.

"The best way you can make it up to me is to pass this test," he remembered himself saying.

At the time, he had thought that her success would make him feel good by validating his skills as a tutor, but as he walked up that lonesome road, surrounded by grass, his mind took him back to a statement he had made to Sha'Tanya after the test.

"I didn't help you because I like tutoring; I helped you because I like you," echoed through his head.

He started to realise that he had become more invested in Sha'Tanya than he had previously allowed himself to admit. He also realised that this investment had given him not only the fortitude to endure his traumatic ordeal, but also the joy he experienced when she excelled.

About ten minutes into his journey, as he began to ascend the steep portion of the hill, he pondered the mission at hand. His new revelation gave him a somewhat different outlook on the deal he had made with Jerome. His investment in Sha'Tanya provided him with a fortitude and eventually a joy, which would not have come from payment; no amount of money could atone for the horror of being drenched in week-old urine. With that in mind, he feared that he was walking into another ordeal, and that the money would not compensate for the resulting trauma.

By the time he reached the top of the hill, five minutes later, he was drenched not only in sweat, but in pessimism. As he walked past a huge sign saying "Welcome to Liberty Heights," and started to walk through the upscale area, he tried to reassure himself.

"This guy's rich, with a maid and a chauffeur," he told himself, "how bad can it be?"

This optimism struggled to survive, however, as Adrian looked around him at the huge mansions, towering over him on each side. Each of them was sequestered behind tall gates and guard walls, giving the area a very impersonal and isolated vibe. The further he penetrated the area, the more it threatened to depress him. With every house he passed, he felt a growing sense that he did not belong there. There wasn't a human being in sight, and the only sounds piercing the stillness of the morning were the barks of dogs—massive dogs. It seemed like every other house possessed one of these monsters; fortunately for Adrian, all of the ones he had seen up to that point were behind closed gates.

After twenty minutes walking through this massive development, Adrian had only reached the fifth mansion on the right, and the tenth mansion overall; he was on route to the seventh on the right, and the thirteenth overall. His ears were still inundated with the sound of barking, but a different sound pierced his ears through all the barking; it was a deep growl, and it sounded closer than his brain told him it should. Adrian looked back to see a huge, brown dog in the smooth road, giving him a sinister stare.

Fear took hold of Adrian with immediate effect. His intellect told him to stay calm and avoid sudden movements, but his heart told him to depart like a train. His intellect succumbed to the weight of his thumping heart forthwith and he took flight like a bullet.

The fifteen-minute hill climb and twenty-minute stroll through the development had resulted in fatigue, but the fear-induced adrenaline he felt at that moment was the prevailing force at play, propelling him beyond his expected physical limits. Nevertheless, each time he glanced behind him, he could see the monster closer than before. As he reached the boundary of the next house, he could see its gate was left open. As he got closer to the gate, he could see a well-kept lawn beyond it, with a medium sized tree. With the monster gaining on him and his heart threatening to evacuate his chest, Adrian darted through the gate, and somehow, scaled the tree like an African green monkey.

As he clung to a branch, the dog jumped up in repeated attempts to reach him, coming close but falling short of its target. This place of safety did not subdue his throbbing heart, but it did allow his intellect to resurface after its sudden casualty. He knew he couldn't stay in the tree indefinitely so he tried to think of an escape path. The only way out of the tree was to return to the lawn, so he needed to dispatch the dog.

"What can I use to dispatch this dog?" he asked himself as he clung tightly to the branch, "the only thing I walked with is my books."

Then, a thought hit him; Sha'Tanya had given him a very strong deodorant spray to mask the urine scent on his bag straps—he had never taken it out of his bag. He carefully removed his right hand from the branch and used it to unzip a side pocket on his backpack. He carefully pulled the spray out of the pocket and un-capped it with his thumb and index finger, while grip-ping it firmly with the remaining digits. He then aimed it quickly at the dog's nose and depressed the nozzle with a vengeance, sending the pungent compressed liquid spraying into the dog's eyes and super-sensitive nose. The dog promptly ceased its jumping and evacu-ated the property, whimpering, and from his perch, Adrian could see it scampering back the way it came.

Adrian jumped down from the tree and retrieved the cover for the spray bottle before making his way towards the gate. By the time he reached the edge of the lawn, his heartrate was attempting to normalise, but that attempt was derailed by a sudden, unexpected shout.

"You," came a stern voice, "you stepped on the wrong property!"

Adrian turned around to see a tall, slender, white man coming down the long driveway with a shotgun in his hands. Adrian threw his hands in the air and suf-fered an instant headache as his heartrate redlined.

"I, I, I'm sorry, sir," he stammered, as his body in-voluntarily shook, "it was the only way I could escape t-t-t-the dog."

Three young men, seemingly between the ages of

sixteen and twenty, ran out of the house and joined the man. Adrian presumed them to be the man's sons as they all looked like smaller replicas of him.

"He was probably robbing one of these houses, Dad," said one of them to the man, confirming Adrian's hypothesis, "that's why the dog ran him."

"Y-y-you got it all wrong," stammered Adrian, "I'm going to a f-f-friend's house. I don't even know where the dog came from."

"You better find that friend's house fast," said the man, raising the shotgun and pointing it in Adrian's direction.

Adrian took flight like an Olympian in the direction of the seventh house, his head competing with his heart for the record of most throbs per minute. In the distance he could hear a voice shouting.

"He can't get off so easily!" cried the voice.

Adrian looked back to see the three young men in pursuit behind him. He was sure his body would fail him; surely his heart and his head could pound neither faster nor harder. Adrenaline seemed to put his feet on autopilot, however, and neither his heart nor his head could stop them as he approached the seventh house.

"Thank goodness the gate is opened," he said to himself as he reached the property.

As he flew past the gatepost, he pressed the doorbell which was affixed to it and proceeded to dart up the long, tiled driveway. At the end of the driveway was a closed garage and a patio on the right, leading to huge French doors. As Adrian mounted the steps to the patio, his three pursuers were already halfway up the driveway. As he entered the patio the doors flew open to reveal Jerome's wiry frame in a t-shirt and short pants.

"Adrian," he cried, excitedly, "I'm so excited for our session I actually answered the door myself."

Jerome then paused and examined the scene before him with puzzlement etched upon his face—three young men running up his driveway and Adrian, winded and wet from head to foot in his own excretion.

"You know this dude, Jerome?" asked one of the boys as he mounted the steps to the patio.

"Yes, this is Adrian," replied Jerome, "he's really smart—gonna help me do a half-decent job on my next test."

The three boys apologized for the misunderstanding and left the property as Jerome invited Adrian inside to use the washroom before meeting his father and starting the session.

Inside the massive washroom, Adrian stared at a huge mirror as he used a washcloth to wipe the sweat from his body.

"This session had better go well," he said to himself as he retrieved the deodorant spray from his pocket, "what I've been through thus far is not worth a hundred dollars—not by a long shot."

As he removed the cap from the deodorant, he paused and looked at it for a moment.

"Sha'Tanya has more than paid her debt; this deodorant not only saved me from that dog, but it also did a pretty good job masking the urine smell," he thought, as he proceeded to spray the deodorant on the crotch of his pants.

He then took a deep breath and prepared to deal with Jerome. Only time would tell whether or not his trip, and his ordeal, were all worth it.

The following Friday, Adrian sat in physics class, next to Sha'Tanya, awaiting the results of a test conducted earlier than week.

"So, how you planning to spend the hundred dollars?" asked Sha'Tanya, as they awaited the arrival of the physics teacher.

"I had planned to put it towards a suit for graduation," started Adrian, "but let's just wait and see what happens with these results before getting too excited."

"You make it sound like the session was a disaster."

"I did a pretty good job, all things considered, but it's up to Jerome to pull it off."

"Well, he ain't trying to ace the test, just to do half-decent," replied Sha'Tanya, with a smile, "so don't feel too pressured."

Just then, Mr. Garnett entered the class and took his usual seat on the edge of the teacher's desk with the results in his hand.

"Good morning class," he started, "as usual, we're gonna start from the bottom and come up."

Anxiety erupted in Adrian's stomach once again. The hundred dollars couldn't make up for the ordeal he had endured, but he would have been especially upset to have gone through it for nothing at all.

"The marks, out of fifty, are as follows," said the teacher, "Akanni Johnson ... zero!"

"What the bird," cried Sha'Tanya, as Akanni performed his usual theatrics and the class laughed, "you did it!"

Mr. Garnett not only called names in order of grade, but also in alphabetical order, which meant that for the first time ever, Jerome didn't get zero. A smile came to Adrian's face and for the first time in days he felt a ray of hope enter his heart as Akanni returned to his seat and the teacher raised the next paper.

"Jerome Atkins," said the teacher, "a half."

Adrian's mouth dropped in shock and bewilderment as Jerome jumped up from his seat with great jubilation.

"Yes," cried Jerome, aloud, "I didn't get zero; I did half-decent!"

Adrian held his head down as the class erupted in both applause and laughter; his headache was back. His head soon popped back up in disbelief, however, as he heard Jerome's voice in his ear.

"My chauffeur will bring your money tomorrow," said Jerome, "you've been most helpful."

THE SEARCH

Adrian stood, staring at a red curtain with anxiety burning in his stomach. He tugged on the jacket of the new suit which enveloped his slim frame, ensuring it was as straight and perfect as possible. Then, taking a deep breath, he propelled himself through the curtain to face the scrutiny which awaited him on the other side.

The curtain gave way to reveal a dark, slim, shapely girl with glossy lips, a powered neck and a hair gel addiction—his friend Sha'Tanya. Next to her stood a short, stout, clear-skinned woman with short curls—the attendant in the Men's Wear section of a city department store. To Adrian's relief, they were both nodding in approval of the purple suit with a white and purple paisley-print shirt, purple fabric shoes and a purple mortarboard.

"Boom!" exclaimed Sha'Tanya.

"The search is over," said the attendant, still nodding, "that's it right there."

Just a couple minutes later, Adrian stood next to Sha'Tanya amongst racks of clothing, now matching his friend's attire—t-shirt, blue jeans and sneakers.

"Thank you for helping me choose my suit," he said to his companion, as they waited for the attendant to package the suit and shoes.

"I don't think I would be graduating without your help, and I definitely wouldn't be the most improved student for the year—just paying my debt," she replied, "besides, you are the vale ... vale-victor—"

"Valedictorian," Adrian corrected her, with a chuckle.

"Right, that," replied Sha'Tanya, slapping Adrian lightly on the shoulder, "if anybody's gotta look good tomorrow evening, it's you."

"Tell me about it," he replied, in a low tone, "there's a lot of pressure on me for this graduation."

"So, that's why you seem so heavy?" she asked, with a critical look. "You feel a little off today."

"Not really," said Adrian, pausing and pondering briefly before taking a folded piece of paper from his pocket and handing it to Sha'Tanya, who started to read it and then looked at Adrian with wide eyes.

"A letter from your father?" she asked, with shock on her face.

"Yup," replied Adrian, "look at the date."

"What the bird! This is five years ago!" cried Sha'Tanya, shaking her head. "I thought you said ..."

"That my father left when I was small and never looked back?" Adrian interrupted with a deceptive calm.

"Yes …," replied Sha'Tanya, pausing with a look of consternation, "but where …?"

"The day you came to get help with your project … I found it by accident while searching the book-shelf," said Adrian, while taking the letter back, "all these years I thought he didn't care, then to find out he wrote to check up on me and my mother kept it from me."

"So, you confronted your mother 'bout it?" asked Sha'Tanya, as the attendant approached them with the suit and shoes packaged.

"Thought about it," Adrian replied, as he took the package and followed the attendant to the cashier, "but I'd prefer to get my info straight from my father."

"Alright, we just gotta find him," said Sha'Tanya, with a gleam in her eyes. "Count me in."

Later that day, Adrian returned home with his new suit, and his new accomplice. From the time they stepped through the front door and into the cosy living room, Adrian's big, brown mother flew out of her bedroom on the right, and demanded to see the outfit. Adrian rushed through the flushed living and dining area to his room, next to his mother's, to change.

Sha'Tanya took this opportunity to retrieve the telephone directory from a bookshelf on the left side of the dining room, before making herself comfortable on the living room suite, with Adrian's mother.

Not long after, Adrian emerged from the bedroom and strutted into the living room in his new threads, causing his mother to become very excited.

"When you insisted on doing this yourself," said

Adrian's mother, "I was worried you might come back here with something dowdy."

"Error," Sha'Tanya exclaimed, assuming a defensive posture, "not with me in the picture; Sha'Tanya Carter does not do dowdy!"

Minutes later, Adrian had changed back into his regular clothes, his mother had recovered from her excitement and Sha'Tanya was joining him in his room to update him on her search. The room was small, but spacious by virtue of the small footprint of a twin-sized bed. The bed was accompanied by a small computer workstation, a chest of drawers and some shelves.

"Bad news," she whispered, as she sat in Adrian's wheeled computer chair and spun around to face him as he sat on the rear edge of the bed, "this dude ain't listed in the directory."

Adrian pondered for a moment.

"My mother should have the number in her little black book," he said, in a semi-excited whisper.

"Little black book?" asked Sha'Tanya, mockingly. "Let me get this straight; she can afford a computer for her son but using a black book instead of a mobile phone?"

"She's old school—hopeless with technology," Adrian explained with a little smile. "I'm guessing I have more of my father's genes."

"So, what's the plan to get this little black book from your mother?" asked Sha'Tanya, as she took a spin in the computer chair.

"You're going to create a diversion," whispered Adrian, outstretching his arms in her direction, "so I can slip into her room and search for the number."

"Create a diversion? How?" whispered Sha'Tanya, bringing the chair to a halt and folding her arms. "I ain't big on acting."

"Ask her to see her arsenal of hair products in the bathroom," said Adrian, with a smug smirk, "and ask her for hairstyle ideas for the graduation."

"But my hair ain't need anything more than two handfuls of gel," she replied, with a ponderous look.

"It's cute that you think so," said Adrian, with a cheeky expression, "but time is ticking away."

Sha'Tanya exited the room, giving Adrian a stare as cold as an ice cube. Moments later, she was in the bathroom with Adrian's mother, and Adrian slipped into his mother's unoccupied bedroom brandishing a ball-point pen. The room was small and cramped. There wasn't much furniture—just a queen-sized bed and a chest of drawers. The room was lit by two windows—one to the front, facing the road, and the other to the right side, facing the side of the house next door. Adrian went immediately to the top right drawer of the chest, and retrieved the small black book. He then sat on the bed and started to go through the book.

After a few minutes, he heard his mother's heavy footsteps approaching the room—but he hadn't found the number as yet.

"I thought Sha'Tanya was keeping her busy," he thought, as the footsteps got closer and anxiety burned within his stomach, "I'm too close to stop now; I can feel it—but I can't get caught."

Seconds later, his mother was entering the room.

"That girl is something else," she muttered to herself, as she sat on the bottom edge of the bed, "I wonder if there are rehab facilities for gel addicts."

Thirty centimetres beneath her posterior was Adrian; he had taken refuge under the bed. Seconds later he had found the number but there was no way to exit the room without being detected.

Over the past year, Adrian had forged a great relationship with his mother; he didn't fear her, but wasn't eager to have a confrontation about the letter so he needed an escape route—but there was none.

As he started to come to terms with the idea that a confrontation was inevitable, there was a sudden, loud noise from outside the house. Adrian's mother got up and ran to the side window, backing the door, to investigate the sound. By the time her attention came back to the room, Adrian was out and entering his own room to find Sha'Tanya spinning in his computer chair.

"You're welcome," she whispered, stopping the chair to face Adrian, as he stood by his bed with his arms folded, "I figured you had to be trapped and hiding, so I cooked up my own diversion to help you get out."

"I wouldn't have been trapped and hiding in the first place if you had kept her in the bathroom like you were supposed to," replied Adrian, in a low voice, accompanied by a cold stare.

"She was looking to wash the gel out of my hair and try a new style," whispered Sha'Tanya, jumping up from the chair in a cantankerous manner.

"That would have been perfect," said Adrian, with

wide eyes.

"Error," replied Sha'Tanya, opening her eyes wider than Adrian's.

"At least you got me out—and I got the number," said Adrian, sitting on the bed as he showed Sha'Tanya the number written in the palm of his hand, "what did you do to create the last diversion?"

"I realised that shark ornament on your dresser was a piggy bank," started Sha'Tanya, still whispering but with great excitement, "so I emptied out some of the money and tossed it through the window to hit the neighbour's galvanised fence."

"You threw my money out the window?" asked Adrian, through his teeth as he stared at Sha'Tanya with wide eyes.

"It was either that or the gaming console on the shelf," replied Sha'Tanya, raising her hands in a defensive posture.

"Error, as you would say" said Adrian, making direct eye contact. "That's a Gladiator 64, given to me as a present for passing my secondary school entrance exam."

"So, I made the right choice, then."

"No—you made the better choice, but there's nothing right about throwing my money out the window," said Adrian, with widened eyes and a stern face. "You're going to go out there and find every cent before the day is over."

"It's cute that you think so," replied Sha'Tanya, with a cheeky expression, "but time is ticking away."

Adrian gave her a stare colder than a snow cone,

but he knew that she was right. Within minutes, they had left the house and were on the grassy main road, at a telephone booth.

As Adrian inserted the coin and dialled the number, anxiety lit up his stomach like a bush fire. He pondered what he would say to his father as he punched in the last digit—then he heard a voice on the other end of the line.

"The number you have dialled has been temporarily disconnected," said the voice. "This is a recording."

Adrian slammed the receiver onto the hook, and banged his head against the phonebooth.

"It's temporarily disconnected," he said in a low tone. "It's like the universe is telling me this is not to be."

"You gonna give up just like that?" asked Sha'Tanya, with her arms folded. "We have the guy's address!"

"His number is disconnected; what if he doesn't live at that address anymore?

"What if he does, and you never bothered to search?" asked Sha'Tanya, staring intently into Adrian's eyes. "You think you could live with yourself?"

Adrian pondered for a moment, then took the letter out of his pocket and unfolded it to check the address—then he dropped his head with a sigh.

"He lives in 'The Dead Sea'," he said, looking at his companion with sad eyes.

"Alright, we could be there before dark."

"But it's 'The Dead Sea'," cried Adrian, "you told me once that it was the worst area in the island; you told me going into 'The Dead Sea' was an 'error' ..."

"That's true," interrupted Sha'Tanya, putting her hand on Adrian's shoulder and staring him in the face, "but I can see how much this means to you, so don't waste time; this is a trip we gotta make."

"I passed through there once, against your advice, and nearly ended up in the hospital," started Adrian, "I can't ask you to come with me; whatever debt you may think you owe me, you paid it by helping me choose my suit."

"This ain't 'bout a debt," replied Sha'Tanya, making direct eye contact, "this is about a friend."

Adrian accepted Sha'Tanya's help and the pair set off for the city again, this time to get a bus to "The Dead Sea". It was only a two-minute walk from the phonebooth to the bus stop, and a bus came quickly. Sha'Tanya approved the bus and half of an hour later they were in the city, in the bus yard, disembarking the bus.

Upon exiting the bus, the pair scanned the bus yard for a bus to "The Dead Sea"—the same route the pair travelled to get to school.

"Boom!" cried Sha'Tanya, pointing in the direction of a bus.

"Oh no!" exclaimed Adrian, following her finger to see a bus glistening brightly in the intense sun, adorned with spoilers and other accessories. The name *Turbulence* was etched into its decorative window tint.

"This is my ride," cried Sha'Tanya, grabbing Adrian's hand and pulling him towards the bus, "'Count Dracula' should be driving, and if 'Red Man' is the conductor today, we won't have to pay a cent."

"No, Sha'Tanya, no," cried Adrian as she pulled him along, "the last time I rode this bus I thought I was going to die!"

"Don't be a baby," she said, with a chuckle, "I've been riding *Turbulence* for six years now and I ain't dead."

"My grandmother had a saying," cried Adrian, as they reached the bus, and Sha'Tanya pulled him through the door, "what doesn't happen in a year can happen in a day."

"I hear my grandmother with that too," replied Sha'Tanya, dragging Adrian through the aisle to the back seat, "but then, she's half-crazy so I ain't know how much stock to put in that."

Adrian had met her grandmother and was of the opinion she was entirely crazy. This observation, however, did not help his cause, so he let that topic die a natural death, as he sat next to Sha'Tanya on the right-hand side of the back seat.

As Adrian sat in the brightly coloured interior, surrounded by intricate airbrushed artwork, the scene around him sparked a memory, and a little smile came across his face.

"What's up with you?" asked Sha'Tanya.

"The last time we sat in the backseat of a popular bus like this, we were going on a date," he said, looking at his companion. "After that train wreck of a date, I would never have thought that three years later I would be here, with you, doing something so personal."

"It's true, that date was awful. My ex-boyfriend tried to beat you," replied Sha'Tanya, with a hearty laugh, "I was surprised you still wanted to be friends after that."

"I didn't—but back then I was too shy to refuse," he said, before putting his hand on top of hers. "Crazy thing is, right now, there's nobody I'd rather do this with."

At that moment, Adrian heard the driver's door open and slam shut and he held the handle on the seat in front of him tightly, bracing himself for what he knew would follow. The engine started, followed by loud music, and then the bus started off with a jolt and zoomed out of the bus yard.

The trip was characterised by speed and slides; as the driver took bends and corners at a high rate of speed, Adrian, Sha'Tanya and the three other passengers in the back seat all slid back and forth towards the left and right.

Count Dracula was, indeed, the driver, but Red Man wasn't conducting, so they had to pay their fares.

In about thirty minutes, after a wild ride, Adrian and Sha'Tanya were disembarking the bus in South Sea Village, colloquially known as "The Dead Sea".

"Time to bail," said Sha'Tanya, as she leapt from her seat and started to move towards the front of the bus.

"Put me by the bus stop there, 'Count'!" she cried, addressing the driver, as Adrian followed with apprehension; he knew what she was about to do.

As the bus reduced speed and approached the bus stop, Sha'Tanya proceeded to descend the steps and leapt out of the bus while it was still moving, hitting the sidewalk in stride. Adrian descended the steps as well, and leapt out of the bus. As his right foot connected with the stationary sidewalk, he knew he had to maintain a stride. As he brought down his left foot, he managed to keep his balance and maintain a stride, while simultaneously reducing speed.

"Not bad," said Sha'Tanya, as he finally brought himself to a halt and the bus sped away without ever stopping, "last time you tried that you nearly burst your face."

"I had a good teacher," said Adrian, with a little grin, remembering their disastrous date.

"At least something good came out of that date," said Sha'Tanya, with a laugh.

"You sure you want to do this?" Adrian asked Sha'Tanya, getting serious as the smell of marijuana filled the air. "Two years ago a thug named 'Bad Nasty' got hurt while chasing me, and his friends tried to maul me; I would hate to run into him or any of his crew."

"Assuming these men even remember you, that would be a long time to hold a grudge," said Sha'Tanya, signalling Adrian to follow her as she started to walk, "follow me."

"You know where you're going?" asked Adrian, sceptically, as he followed.

"Yeah, my ex-boyfriend went to school out here," replied Sha'Tanya, "still likes to hang out in the area."

"Wait, hold up," cried Adrian, halting in his tracks, "you mean the same ex-boyfriend that tried to pummel me?"

"Be cool," said Sha'Tanya, with a smile, "whatever

happens, we would face it together—but for now, just be cool and act like you belong here."

The pair set off walking through a rugged landscape, accented with mostly dilapidated houses, headed for the street denoted in the heading of the letter. As they walked, they passed much activity—men playing dominoes and road tennis, children riding bicycles and women having arguments. Activity-wise, the area wasn't very different from Sha'Tanya's district, and from Adrian's perspective, she was oozing with a relaxed confidence as she stepped. Adrian found his confidence in the fact that he was walking with her.

That confidence was soon put to the test, as the pair approached a dark man of medium height, with cornrowed hair, walking in the opposite direction. As he approached the pair, Adrian could see his eyes fixed on them. His intent, persistent stare sent a shiver down Adrian's spine, triggering memories of his last encounter in "The Dead Sea". As the man passed adjacent to them, he locked eyes with Adrian, who quickly broke the lock and kept his head forward. As he kept his visual focus forward, Adrian tuned his ears backward, hearing the man's footsteps continuing into the distance as he progressed. This brought him some relief, but it broke his confidence. Sha'Tanya may have been comfortable in that environment, but should an altercation ensue, history had taught him that she wouldn't be very helpful.

Not long after, the pair entered another street, with much less activity and mostly abandoned houses. There, they saw another figure walking towards them—a tall, dark, muscular male.

"Oh boy," said Sha'Tanya.

"What?" cried Adrian.

"It's my ex-boyfriend—Dashawn," she replied in a low voice, "just be cool."

"That's easy for you to say," Adrian muttered, "you ain't the one he tried to beat."

Dashawn altered his trajectory and headed directly into their path, halting their progression.

"Well, well, well," said Dashawn, putting his hand on Sha'Tanya's shoulder, "if it ain't Sha'Tanya—and the thief that carried away my sweet girl."

"He ain't my boyfriend, but even if he was, he couldn't carry away something you did … not … have," said ShaTanya, with attitude. "And another thing—your hand … on my shoulder—error!"

"Deciding to finish this relationship—that was the error," said Dashawn, with a cruel look, as he squeezed her shoulder.

"Ow!" cried Sha'Tanya, to Adrian's dismay.

Adrian rushed forward and pushed Dashawn backward, off Sha'Tanya—a very uncharacteristic action for him to take.

Dashawn quickly lunged forward and attacked Adrian, putting him in a headlock. Adrian felt powerless and humiliated as Sha'Tanya looked on.

"I' real' sorry 'bout all of this," she said, before dashing off past him.

"She's fleeing the scene like she always does," Adrian thought to himself, his heart sinking even further.

Suddenly, he heard a cry of pain from Dashawn,

who immediately released his grip. Adrian spun around to see Sha'Tanya on Dashawn's back, biting him on his ear. Sha'Tanya jumped off and signalled to Adrian to run, and the two dashed off in the direction they were originally heading. As they ran, Adrian looked back to see Dashawn initiating pursuit.

"I can't believe you bit him," he cried to Sha'Tanya, as they approached a blind corner at the end of the street.

"I can't believe you pushed him," she replied, as they turned the corner with speed.

Suddenly, their motion was interrupted as they ran head on into a group of three thuggish looking men, knocking themselves and a tall, clear man with un-kempt hair to the ground.

"These children can't be serious," shouted one of the other two men, as Dashawn came flying around the corner, almost running into the group as well.

Adrian was gripped with fear; there were three thugs before him and one behind him.

"That was a big error, Sha'Tanya!" shouted Dashawn, ignoring the crowd and gripping her by the neck.

Before Adrian could respond, the man who had been knocked down, flew up and punched Dashawn in the face, knocking him off Sha'Tanya and to the ground.

"No, big man," he shouted, "you can't be roughing up my girl, Sha'Tanya!"

"Red Man!" cried Sha'Tanya, with great excite-ment. "I thought you would be conducting *Turbulence* but I' so glad to run into you here."

Dashawn picked himself up off the ground and proceeded to flee.

"Don't let that fool get off so easy, men," cried Red Man to his companions, "he needs messing up!"

The other two men dashed off behind Dashawn, as Sha'Tanya formally introduced Adrian to the off-duty conductor.

"You know someone from this area named Anderson Manning?" Sha'Tanya asked Red Man.

"I don't know 'bout a 'Anderson' from out here," he replied, after taking a moment to think, "but I think there's a man in Milton Street they call 'Manning'."

Sha'Tanya and Adrian looked at each other, each with gleaming eyes—Milton Street was the address on the letter.

As the pair resumed their journey, Adrian had renewed vigour, surer than ever before that they were on the right track.

As they left Red Man and turned into the next street, they passed a group of four shirtless men hanging out on the steps of an abandoned house. As they passed the men, Adrian heard one of them utter a question which sent a flaming arrow straight through his chest and down into his stomach.

"That boy ain't look familiar, Bad Nasty?" said the voice.

"Just play it cool," said Sha'Tanya, in a low tone, as they continued to walk.

"If anything happens, I'll run towards Milton Street," Adrian whispered back, "I want you to go for help; don't get caught up in my mess."

Then they heard a voice from behind them ordering them to turn around.

"Remember," whispered Adrian, as they slowly turned around, "worst case scenario, you go for help."

A tall, dark, shirtless man, with braided hair and a scar across his right cheek, rose from the step and made eye contact with Adrian.

"It is you," shouted the man, pointing to the scar on his face, "'Ringo' lost probation because of you—and you scrawled up my face, big man!"

The man charged at Adrian, who took off like lightning, leaving Sha'Tanya behind, as they had discussed. Based on the number of footsteps he could hear behind him, he knew that he was being pursued not only by Bad Nasty, but by his companions also. There was other activity on the street, but everyone just cleared the way and watched; no one intervened.

Adrian's heart was in overdrive; he remembered his previous encounter with Bad Nasty and his friends, from which he had narrowly escaped. The fear from his memory seemed to merge with the fear he was presently experiencing, amplifying it.

As Adrian continued to run, he saw a sign saying "Milton Street", and he dashed through the street to which the sign pointed, only to see that past the houses, it led to a dead end—a solid brick wall.

Adrian slowed his pace in despair, as Bad Nasty entered the street and jumped through the air, knocking him to the ground from behind.

Bad Nasty rose, allowing Adrian to turn his body

to face his attacker, who promptly gripped him by the shirt and pull him to his feet.

The other men gathered around to witness the retribution Bad Nasty was preparing to execute.

"Every time I look in a mirror, I remember you," cried Bad Nasty, with a cruel look. "You can't scrawl up men face, and walk 'bout like nothing ain't happened."

Adrian had a response for his attacker, but he couldn't utter it; he had no control of his shaking body.

"Been waiting two years to mess you up so you better brace you'self, big man," said Bad Nasty, as he raised his hand in a fist to pound Adrian's face.

Adrian closed his eyes tightly, on the brink of hyperventilation, awaiting the impending pain, when he heard a loud voice intervening.

"Drop that hand before I level you, Bad Nasty!" shouted the voice.

Bad Nasty lowered his hand and turned his head towards the voice, as Adrian opened his eyes to see who had spoken. There, at the mouth of Milton Street, was a dark man of medium height, with cornrowed hair—the same man that had stared at Adrian so intently when he first entered "The Dead Sea". Sha'Tayna stood behind him, looking on.

"This ain't concern you, Manning," shouted Bad Nasty, as Adrian and Sha'Tanya made eye contact, both with wide eyes and dropped jaws.

"It concerns me 'cause that is my son you' looking to mess up!" shouted Manning, waving his arms threateningly.

The three men that had followed Bad Nasty stepped backward at the revelation that Manning was Adrian's father, but Bad Nasty defiantly stepped forward. Manning charged at him, triggering him to advance forcefully as well. The two men met soon thereafter, with Bad Nasty swinging a fist at Manning, who ducked under it, and ploughed into him, lifting him from the ground, and then reuniting him with it in a body slam.

When the other three men saw Bad Nasty slammed head-first into the road, they evacuated the area, as their friend picked himself up in a daze. When he saw that his companions had fled, he groggily followed suit, leaving Adrian to get some answers.

Sha'Tanya explained that shortly after Adrian had fled, she ran into Manning, who stopped her and asked where her friend was. She took a chance asking him for help, never suspecting that he was the man they were looking for.

"When I passed you the first time, I was staring 'cause you looked so much like my son," said Manning to Adrian. "When I ran into your friend, I was on my way back to find you; when she said 'Adrian', that's when I was sure."

Adrian was inundated with emotions; he was relieved to complete the search and happy to find his father but curiosity, confusion and even a little anger were also in the mix.

"Why did you abandon me?" Adrian asked, with water settling in his eyes. "What was wrong with me?"

"Nothing was wrong with you, everything 'bout you was perfect," cried Manning, gripping Adrian by the shoulders, right there in the middle of the street, with neighbours curiously peeping through their windows, "I was the problem!"

"Huh?"

"My father was a horrible father," started Manning, "and out of the blue, I had a son, but I never had a real father, so I didn't think I was good enough to father you."

"Explain this," said Adrian, producing the letter for his father.

"You ain't supposed to have this," said Manning, after glancing at the paper. "Around the time you were transitioning to secondary school, I sent that letter, hoping to be a part of your life again."

"I don't understand," interrupted Adrian, with a perplexed look.

"After I sent the letter, I called and asked your mother not to give it to you," he said, returning the letter to Adrian. "I still had some issues in my life—so I sent a gaming console instead, and told your mother not to tell you who it was from."

"The Gladiator 64," cried Adrian, in shock, "I can't believe that was from you."

"I sent a lot of things since then, like your computer desk, and the money for your new suit."

"Look, I didn't need you to send me stuff," said Adrian, with passion, "I just wanted a father."

"You might be better off without me."

"Please," pleaded Adrian, "at least come to my

graduation tomorrow. You don't need an invitation; I'll iron it out with the principal."

"Let me think 'bout it," said Manning, "but it's starting to get late; let me take you and your friend back to the bus stop before it gets dark."

The trip back to town was a silent one; Adrian was lost in his thoughts. For years, he believed that he wasn't good enough to keep his father's interest. While he had come a long way in gaining a sense of self-worth, he now realised that this condition wasn't unique to him; a lot of people felt like they weren't good enough—even his father.

About an hour after the encounter with Bad Nasty, Adrian and Sha'Tanya were back in the city, in the bus yard, preparing to part ways and head to their respective homes.

"Whatever the outcome," said Adrian, "I want to thank you for your support today."

"Don't mention it," replied Sha'Tanya, "and don't get sappy on me."

"Oh!" Adrian exclaimed, as Sha'Tanya turned to leave. "I almost forgot; I have something for you."

Adrian reached into his pocket and pulled out a hundred-dollar bill.

"I was saving this to help buy my suit, but my mother—I mean, my father—gave me all the money I needed," he said, as he handed the money to Sha'Tanya. "I want you to take this to the hairdresser tomorrow, and get something as bold and special as you are—no gel.

"This is too much," said Sha'Tanya, with water settling in her eyes, "whatever debt you may think you owe me …"

"This ain't 'bout a debt," Adrian interrupted, making direct eye contact, "this is about a friend."

Sha'Tanya hugged Adrian tightly, with tears running down her cheeks.

"Now who's getting sappy?" Adrian whispered in her ear.

For once, she didn't have a witty retort. She just kissed him on the cheek and departed with his gift. In that moment, Adrian realised how valuable she had become in his life; without her encouragement and tenacity, he would never have found his father.

Five years prior, he had fallen in love with her tight uniform and glistening hair. A couple years later, he finally got to take her on a disastrous date, which ended that infatuation sharply. Now, surprisingly, that infatuation had resurrected, not because of her clothes, shape and hair, but because of who she was. He resolved that directly after the graduation ceremony, he would ask her to be his girlfriend—but first, he had to get through his graduation, and his valedictorian speech.

The following evening, at the graduation, Principal Harding introduced the valedictorian as none other than Adrian Manning. As applause filled the air, Adrian stood, staring at a red curtain with anxiety burning in his stomach. He tugged on the jacket of the new suit which enveloped his slim frame, ensuring it was as straight and perfect as possible. Then, taking a deep breath, he propelled himself through the curtain to face the scrutiny which awaited him on the other side.

THE SEARCH

The curtain gave way to reveal a sea of people, all applauding and admiring him for his accomplishment. As he made his way to the podium, in his new purple suit, with a purple mortarboard on his head, he scanned the large crowd. All of these people were there cheering him on, but the one person he was looking for was his father. As he reached the podium, he shook the hand of the principal, a tall, clear man with an Adam's apple reminiscent of a goitre, and a shiny bald head; after years of valiant battle against recession, his hairline had perished, never to be seen again. As the principal exited the stage, Adrian pulled a piece of paper out of his pocket, and unfolded it on the podium to make a startling discovery; he had picked up the letter from his father instead of his speech. As the crowd restlessly awaited the commencement of his speech, Adrian's anxiety began to turn to panic—then his eyes fell on his father, seated in the crowd. The hundreds of people who had applauded him just a moment ago—the very attention he had craved for so long—had failed to make him feel as valuable as this one individual did, and in that moment, the panic and anxiety subsided.

"Good evening, fellow students, parents and faculty of Angela Miller Secondary," he started, "I stand here, before you, because of an academic accomplishment, but what is an accomplishment, if not the culmination of a journey?

"Therefore, this evening, I speak not of the accomplishment, but of the journey," he continued, with conviction as his gaze fell on his big, brown mother, who was clad in an Indian inspired outfit, "I have been

Adrian at large—running far and wide in search of attention and popularity."

Adrian paused briefly, smiling as his gaze fell upon his dark, chubby, flat nosed friend, Alex.

"I found that popularity, and everyone knew the name, Adrian, at last—but the search was not satisfied," he continued, looking at his clear, hump-nosed friend, Jay, "something was still missing, and I became Adrian at loggerheads—at odds with people around me, but really at odds with myself."

Adrian paused, staring at his father intently for a moment.

"You see, a search is pointless until you truly know what it is you are searching for," he continued, with passion, commanding the attention of the hushed auditorium, "some of us are looking for popularity, some are looking for romance, others are looking for a sense of purpose; I've sought all of those things on this journey, but the turning point came when I realised that the thing I was really searching for, was self-worth."

At that point, his eyes fell on Sha'Tanya, adorned in a beautiful, iridescent, sequinned gown. Her hair was braided in long extensions, and wrapped upwards into a nice style.

"I'm truly grateful for the awesome support I've had on this journey," he said, lowering his voice a bit, "the people who have helped me to see my own self-worth; without that, this accomplishment would mean nothing."

At that point, Adrian's gaze panned the full group of his peers.

"Fellow students," he continued, as he gestured in their direction, "regardless of your academic results, as you go into new institutions, make new friendships and even evolve existing ones," he said, allowing his wandering eyes to rest on Sha'Tanya, "the greatest qualification you can carry with you is your own certificate of self-worth; that will free you to accomplish anything else."

Adrian looked down at the open letter on the podium, and took a deep breath before lifting his head to the audience one last time.

He fixed his eyes on his father, hearing his words echoing in his mind, "Nothing was wrong with you, everything 'bout you was perfect."

"In closing," said Adrian, addressing the audience for the last time, "for years, I've been trapped in an endless search, but this evening, I stand before you, Adrian … at liberty."

Adrian then folded the letter and exited the stage to a standing ovation.

Get all the books in the *Adrian* Series

www.marioherbert.com

**Coming next in
the *Adrian* universe**

Sha'Tanya
UNLEASHED

A prequel to Adrian at Large

See the synopsis on the next page

Sha'Tanya UNLEASHED

Thirteen-year-old Barbadian schoolgirl, Sha'Tanya Carter, lives in a simpler time, where corporal punishment abounds, and DVDs are the preferred medium for watching movies. She has no lack of confidence, and no reservations about pointing out when others are in error. She's a pretty popular girl; she rides only the most popular buses, has very loyal friends and everybody who is somebody knows her.

What could such a girl yearn for? At face value, it's a boy, but could it be something more? Could it be that she really wants to be grownup? What happens when someone with such motivations is left to their own devices?

Questionable decisions abound, bringing Sha'Tanya—and those around her—face to face with adventure, treachery and ultimately, peril.

Who is really for her? Who is really against her? Could it be that she is the source of all her biggest troubles? Find out, as you follow the adventures of Sha'Tanya, unleashed.